IS A HALF-FORMED THING
ESSER BOHEMIANS
HOTEL

SPR

We hope you enjoy this book. Please return or renew it by the due date.

You can renew it at www.norfolk.gov.uk/libraries or by using our free library app.

Otherwise you can phone 0344 800 8020 - please have your library card and PIN ready.

You can sign up for email reminders too.

30 D0177403

NORFOLK COUNTY COUNCIL
LIBRARY AND INFORMATION SERVICE

A GIRL

THE LE

STRANG

# MOUTHPIECES

Eimear McBride

faber

First published in 2020 by
Faber & Faber Ltd
Bloomsbury House
74–77 Great Russell Street
London WC1B 3DA

This paperback edition first published in 2021

Typeset by Faber & Faber Limited
Printed and bound by CPI Group (UK) Ltd, Croydon, CR0 4YY

A CIP record for this book
is available from the British Library

ISBN 978-0-571-36581-4

FSC
www.fsc.org
MIX
Paper from
responsible sources
FSC® C020471

2 4 6 8 10 9 7 5 3 1

For Éadaoin

# MOUTHPIECES

# The Adminicle Exists

*Bare stage. One female voice.*

VOICE:

I saw you. I saw you. I got you by the shirt. I
stopped you walking into the road.
Blue skies.
Greyish High Road
WIDE
Children playing on bikes.
I held tight on. And on to you tight. You didn't
know the stops any more.
Roaring at the driver you calamatised the bus.
I pressed you to the pole. My foot entrapped
your foot. There was no choice but stay.
WAR MEMORIAL
TFC
CHEAP FLIGHTS TO ANTIGUA
SEND MONEY CHEAP HERE
TESCO
TESCO
TESCO
LONDON UNDERGROUND
STOP
The state of that – cigarette burning on a pile
of sick.

I pulled you by the shirt. You did not object.
Down into the intestines. The escalator
descended. You stood notably upright like
demonstrating sane, but I kept your cuff
between my finger and thumb. I watched you
on the platform. I watched you by the train.
I let you get onto it first. Indignantly you
eschewed a seat. I did not press. The doors
juddered shut and the windows soon went
black.
I have you. I have you. Across bumps and
irregular speed.
You stumbled with momentum, despite
anticipating stops. You grabbed on to me. I
tried to talk you down from the shouts, but
you only half-heeded my plea.
[*small voice, like inner thought*] I hate how you
scream like a child. My palms itch red to slap
you quiet.
I should not do that though and, at least, know
not to do.
But all the Londoners made out not to see,
for which I blessed their maligned courtesy
and restraint. Even more as I pushed you – at
Highbury and Islington – away. You need

6

though, you need it. No don't, I say, I don't want to kiss you now. Here. [*small voice, like inner thought*] Ever again.

'I NEED TO. I NEED TO. YOU KNOW IT CALMS ME DOWN.'

Stop shouting. [*small voice, like inner thought*] Please stop shouting.

Alright. Anything to

Slither. Your fucking tongue. Getting itself right into my mouth so you will feel better and I will feel?

[*small voice, like inner thought*] I will be?

But this is happening to you, not me. My body the locator of your self-discipline, it seems.

Even so though – enough!

EVERYTHING STOPS. And that is the Tube, not me.

Get off now. This is our stop. It takes all my ingenuity to catch and drag you off while you, like a UFO, boggle at the platform then test the ground beneath your feet.

Up the stairs, the many stairs. We went to the outside once more.

Lively, all this life around. Consumers' pretty things. If we had any money, if we had

anything, we'd live like this too.
Ha ha ha, you shout:
'Shoppers! What wonders you possess!
What credit cards! What overdrafts!'
I see what you see, and my pockets are as light,
but the salvage remains on me.
So.
Never mind all this.
Listen.
No listen.
I mean it.
Follow me. Follow me.

I didn't even know which road I went to. But I
know it now.

Let me in. Let me in. Let me in. Let us in.
Pleasepleasepleasepleaseplease.
And there is respite.
Someone opens the door. She says 'Can I help?'
I say I have nowhere else to go and she says
'Yes. Come in. Come on in. If he'd like to take
a seat just there.'
Sit down.
Sit.

Please just sit.
Please just sit while I explain what's happened.
Just sit.
No sit.
Please just fucking sit.
I won't be a minute, okay?
I gave it up. You up to them. All the details.
I had no shame. Your lost articulation. Your
lost rag. I was sympathetic. Enlightening. I
was not angry. I was a benevolent master of
your domain and, even when they pressed for
everything, never said I feared you'd kill me in
my sleep.
'So,' they said, with smiles, 'why don't you
come through?'
'She'll wait here,' they said 'You'll wait for him,
won't you?'
I'll be right here, I said, I'll wait. Go with them.
I'll see you later. Everything will be fine.
My own lies twist but they can't listen.
[*small voice, like inner thought*] Jesus Christ lock
him away.
You agreed then, drawing to your height.
Showing your dignity, as you imagined it. You
would provide information, even seek their

9

advice. And they took you out.

[*small voice, like inner thought*] THANK GOD.

But also, not. And also . . . not very far.

The vigil then. I am well-behaved. I smile
when smiled at. I draw no attention to myself.
I just wait here now, as expected. I am a very
good citizen. I am cognisant of what they're
doing for you so, by extension, me. I make no
attempt to shirk. I shoulder all responsibility.
And I don't just [*small voice, like inner thought*]
want to run.

White crossed light.

Your voice somewhere.

Magazines to be read.

Other side of the wall.

Red squares and grey squares.

Paper thin.

In my seat.

Is that you screaming?

Tea?

I hear.

Thanks very much.

Maddening, maddening in your distress.

I dream of smoking.

Help me HELP ME. Help me Help me.

My kingdom for a cigarette.

But.

The door opens.

The door closes.

And then there are more.

Rats in traps.

Fish in nets.

Heads in hands.

Hands on faces.

Irises dilated.

Leading or led.

'Tell me your name.' Over and again.

'Tell me your name.'

'Tell me your name.'

'I REALLY NEED A NAME FOR YOU . . .
PLEASE.'

And I am concealed behind their distress. I
take pride in keeping my own to myself. My
face wears pity even if feeling disgust. Pull
yourselves together, I almost shout. But I do
not. Of course, I don't do that.

And.

The door opens.

The door closes.

And then there are more.

The angry.
The incapacitated.
The full of shit.
The too many drugs.
The too much drink.
The fatally confused.
The terminally entitled.
The poor.
The lonely.
The hungry.
The sad.
The fucked up on the street.
The fucked up in the head.
The hopeless.
The helpless.
The feckless.
Myself.
I am here as well.
Then.
An inner door opens. A man walks through.
Your voice screaming somewhere, other side
of the wall. I listen with care. I separate your
words out.
'AM I CRAZY? AM I CRAZY? ARE YOU
GOING TO LOCK ME UP?'

But when he smiles at me, I smile back. You
may expect me to smile. I will also be good-
mannered. I will not shout or show distress.
I'll be pleasant for hours. I am built for this. I
possess the stamina for shit. For a woman, I am
very sturdily constituted – which is really just
as well as this could happen again and again
and again. To you. And me.
The door opens.
The door closes.
And then there are more.
A woman slaps her daughter.
A man curses at his wife.
A girl vomits on the floor.
A girl wipes it up.
A boy throws a magazine.
A man slams his fist.
A pile of people pile on him.
I hardly jump. It's only violence after all.
And I hear you scream the other side of the
wall.
I hear you not scream the other side of the
wall.
I am very sick of your problems.
I hope they will lock you up.

I insist I hope they will let you out.
Really, I hope they will let me out.
I don't know what to do.


I'd like some different magazines.
A sharp blow to the head.
Some fucking family around to offer me a
hand.
I would like to be wasted.
I would like
I would
like
Who fucking cares what you'd like? You stupid
FUCKING CHILD.


A door opens.
A door closes.
And then there are more.


I don't want to look at these people. I can't
believe I'm here. I don't want to be one of
them.
'Hey you! Hey you! Stop fucking watching
me!'
Hey yourself! What the fuck does it matter

what I see? Just get back to whichever useless
fuck-up you brought in and leave me alone
OKAY?
'Okay, sorry, I didn't mean anything by it.'
Fuck you.

'There now.'
Don't there me.
'Just sit back down. How long have you been
here?'
Since the early morning.
'Have you been told to wait?'
It's expected I will.
'What have they said?'
They haven't said anything. I've been told
nothing at all.
'I'm sorry about that. I'll see what I can do.'
'He's doing much better.
He's calmed down a lot.
We're just getting him tidied back up.'
Tidied up, why?
'Stuff he did to his clothes . . . stuff he did to
his head.'
And now?
'He's fine.'

Will he stay that way?
'We're hopeful but . . . we can't promise
anything.'
No . . . of course not.
'He's lucky to have you.'
He is.


The door opens.
The door closes.
And then there is you.
Less wild-eyed, saying I'm alright. Saying I'm
much better. Saying everything will be fine.
And they tell me you'll need a lot of rest. They
ask me to be responsible for ensuring you get
it.
'Now, you'll make sure he gets that, won't you?'
I'll handle everything.
We smile at each other.
They offer you to me.
Hi, I say How're you doing?
You say, Sorry about earlier. Sorry for
everything.
I am very glad to see you calm but
[*small voice, like inner thought*] I wonder if you'll
kill me tonight?

And
We take each other's hands.
I say Thank you very much.
I sign the forms.
I smile at the receptionist.
I make apologetic eyes to the person I
cursed at.
Then I find our way out onto Marshall Street.
I ask how you feel and you say you are
exhausted.
Well, I suggest, I've about three quid left, do
you want to get something to eat?

*Black.*

An Act of Violence

*Bare stage. One figure 'E', female. 'A' is a voice, officious, loud, coming from all angles.*

A: It was an act of violence.

E: It was not.

A: A wound was inflicted?

E: More than one.

A: Scratches?

E: Several.

A: Slices?

E: The same.

A: The knife penetrated the skin?

E: It went all the way in.

A: You saw it?

E: With my own two eyes.

A: Then it was an act of violence.

E: I disagree.

A: There was blood?

E: Some.

A: Screaming?

E: Too.

A: Distress?

E: Certainly.

A: Exhibited by all present?

E: An atmosphere accrued.

A: Elaborate, if you would.

E: They were tired.

A: Noticeably?

E: Conspicuously so.

A: Elaborate.

E: Exhaustion impeded their view.

A: They did view, however?

E: They did.

A: It attracted attention?

E: Obviously.

A: Disapproval?

E: A bit.

A: Which became verbalised?

E: Gradually.

A: But rapidly enough?

E: Rapidly enough for what?

A: To bring about intervention?

E: There was none of that.

A: Intolerable disinterest.

E: They were exhausted.

A: That is no excuse.

E: It is not offered as such.

A: As nothing was offered.

E: Nothing was asked.

A: But is now.

E: And now, is answered.

A: Most unsatisfactory.

E: To whom?

A: To me.

E: Acting upon what authority?

A: That of an interested party.

E: Which interest?

A: In the interest of clarity: that all things should
be made clear.

E: To whom?

A: The attentive.

E: Who are?

A: We.

E: The collective?

A: Yes.

E: The body?

A: Indeed.

E: Of which you represent?

A: The ear.

E: Not the mouth?

A: When necessity requires.

E: Such as now?

A: It was an act of violence.

E: About which no doubt may be entertained?

A: The evidence is obvious.

E: If disregarding my statement?

A: Perhaps your view was obscured.

E: I could see perfectly.

A: You allow no margin of error?

E: It is expected I should?

A: Common sense dictates.

E: Whose?

A: Come come, there is no occurrence upon which doubt cannot be thrown.

E: Shall not be thrown.

A: Be that as it may.

E: A substantial assertion.

A: A simple fact.

E: Inexhaustibly reliable?

A: Empirically accurate.

E: And of impeccable provenance?

A: My credentials are intact.

E: As representative of the body?

A: I pride myself.

E: Mouth or ear?

A: It was an act of violence.

E: It was not.

A: The knife went in?

E: To the hilt.

A: The organs sustained damage?

E: Anecdotally, yes.

A: You did not intercede?

E: I did not.

A: Offered no assistance?

E: The difficulty was no longer mine to resolve.

A: But a difficulty existed?

E: Undoubtedly.

A: Yet you remained unconcerned?

E: My concerns were elsewhere.

A: Not with the preservation of life?

E: Ummm . . .

A: The protection of estate?

E: The estate of his body?

A: All bodies are the same.

E: I would say not.

A: Or are not, any longer.

E: As the case may be.

A: As has proved the case.

E: If it is as you say.

A: I do.

E: The mouth says.

A: And nothing dissents.

E: The ears?

A: They cannot speak for themselves.

E: Eyes neither.

A: Just as you say.

E: We have reached an impasse.

A: But not the end.

E: Well then, ask more.

A: There was an act of witness?

E: In what way?

A: You saw.

E: The sighted see.

A: To what end?

E: Needlessly.

A: Accurately?

E: Hopelessly.

A: Powerlessly?

E: Inevitably.

A: Inevitably?

E: In this case, yes.

A: So, there was an act of violence?

E: Ummm . . .

A: There were scratches?

E: Yes.

A: Slashes?

E: Yes.

A: The knife penetrated skin?

E: I do not deny it.

A: Organs were damaged?

E: I am led to believe.

A: Others present exhibited alarm?

E: They did, perhaps even distress.

A: The victim requested assistance?

E: Yes.

A: Begged for mercy?

E: True.

A: This request was ignored?

E: By me.

A: The others present too?

E: Some horror was expressed, but a deaf ear was the favoured consensus.

A: It was an act of violence.

E: Of joy.

A: In the misfortune of another?

E: I did not say schadenfreude.

A: But it was avoidable?

E: It may once have been.

A: It was an act of violence.

E: It was not an act.

A: What then?

E: Let's say, an end.

A: For the victim?

E: Yes.

A: For the perpetrator?

E: That too.

A: For all concerned?

E: Close enough.

A: Especially for him though?

E: For, but not especially.

A: For who else then?

E: [*non-committally*] Oh, you know.

*Black.*

# The Eye Machine

*Bare black stage. Eight feet above stage level, a rostrum. On it, a woman, clearly visible, strapped to a board. Arms and head strapped, to render her immobile. She does not attempt to remain immobile but does not actively struggle against the restraints. Delivery rapid but comprehensible. Human.*

EYE: What if it couldn't? I? What if she? What if she said fifteen things, all in a row. Five things. Ten. What if there was some noise? A loud crash. A bang. It can be very distracting, you know. Di-stressing. De-mystification is also a thing, you know. After all, there is the large and small. There is the broad and slim. Narrow. Lacking in shape. There is the long and the short of it. The shorter. The very short. What if she. I. Didn't know how to say it. Didn't know how to say? Didn't know. What if it was right there? A bit to the side? At an abstruse angle? In the wings? If wings went. Or go? If there was no stop and go? If there was go only? If there was only stop. No. Stop. Go. No. Stop. And what if she didn't think this was like anything? If there were no metaphors. Antonyms. Metonyms. If there was only what it was, and the story was told at the same time it was. If there was no story. If there was only is? If this was the one way. The only way. Only the way. If she felt that her legs were there. Hands were there. If her face and head and all the other bits just sat. In time. In the here and now. The then and there. If she could not see around the corner. If there was no corner to see around. If the corner, or not, was the end of it all. But if the corner was the be-all and end-all, of it all. Of everything. If there was no everything only this thing and that was all things. If she thought like that. If she thought that. If there was no getting to. If there was only is. If is, is the thing she liked to think except there is no like and there is no think, there is only is. There is no only. There is, is. Is, is all there is? If she decided nothing was in the offing because nothing was in the offing. There was no offing, eventually or inevitably or ever. If there was no ever. If there is only is. But not only. Just is. Here. Now. Continually. Thus far and as far ahead as the eye can see. If the eye can see. If the eye only is. If the eye just is, without interpretation, intervention of the brain or even emotion to bring it on. To pursue it from itself to whatever is next. What if she is stuck. Brittle. Or stuck. Fast. Or stuck. Hard. But not any of these things. Only settled forever. Except there is no settled and there is no forever. If she cannot find a way out because there is no way. Because there is no out. Because there is no because. Just is. On and on and on. If the eye cannot look at itself. If the eye cannot look at anything else. If the eye cannot look. If it just belongs to a system of seeing which it cannot impact, interpret, depict, construe, transpose, contextualise. That's the thing. If there is a thing. If the eye – God help us. If the eye – God help us. Sees infinitely, interminably what it is shown. If it knows only what it is shown. If it is created from what is shown. Can be only what it is shown. And what it is shown is

Fat girls

Thin girls

Sex girls

Rape girls

Hit girls

Killed girls

Dead girls

Lost girls

Stupid girls

Wild girls
Mothers
Martyrs
Pigs on sticks.
Desiccated.
Dehydrated.
Detested.
Grandmothers hanging from the goalposts of
their pasts.
Women as animals.
Meat women.
Leg women.
Rumps.
Tits.
Mouths agog 'gape 'ghast.
Willing.
Innocent.
Wrecked.
Racked.
Hopeless.
Plain.
More beautiful than a summer's day.
A red, red, rose.
A bird in flight.
More ugly than a

34

She
Girl
Women, woman
Female
Chromosome
Hormone
Hairy leg.
There for your vaginas and
Your bras
And
Your breasts.
For your high-heel shoes
And tampons
And tights
And make-up bags
And made-up fights.
We see you.
Saw
We
From the blender.
Buzz.
In a body.
I am
Forever.
Buzz buzz.

Engendered, 'dangered, entreated.
Damn!
You are looking, right the way through.
Looking at me.
Looking. Look.
Staring at
Undressing me.
Hitting
Fucking
Teaching me to
Cry
Fight
Puke
Fall
Fail
Finesse.
Finish what I started.
Finish what you started.
Owe you.
Owe you
EVERYTHING.
Mouth up.
Mouth down.
Mouth open.
Legs open.

Wings clipped.
Free to be filled with
Dumped with
Sumped
Damped down.
At liberty always to see
Ha ha ha.
I see.
Saw.
Seen.
Everything.
And you for
And you as
And you were.
And she has been.
And they will be
Or will not be.
Looked on
Cast to
Glanced at
Picked!
Fucked.
Forgiven.
Fucked.
Forgotten.

Or not.
Or not forgotten.
Or not forgiven.
Right the way to.
All the way to
Kingdom come down here and get a look at this
And be.
And be not.
What I will.
Or choose.
Or wish not.
And I am.
Amid.
The outside of.
The leaching from.
And lurching out of.
Reaching through.
And being.
Because of.
Quaint ideas and quiet quotas.
Qualitative concerns and quantitative problems.
Difficulties – say 'Difficulties' or someone will
complain.
Difficulties.
Difficulties.

Difficulty that
I am.
In the
Ether
Earth
In the underground.
In the vaults of cracked teeth.
The smite of lungs.
Black eyes.
Burnt flesh.
Carved and dined.
Damage.
I am.
I am that.
Damage.
To the scope.
To the scape.
To a whole life's work.
Circe.
Satan.
In the breathing.
In the blood.
In the long mellow night.
From the moment I woke.
Spanish flu and fly, the same.

I am.
And she.
And I am.
A powerful eye staring out from the depths of
your machine.

*Black.*